This Little Tiger Book Belongs To:

For Adele and Samuel
~ IG

For Rebecca
~ TW

LITTLE TIGER PRESS
An imprint of Magi Publications
1 The Coda Centre, 189 Munster Road, London SW6 6AW
This paperback edition published 2002
First published in Great Britain 2001
Text © 2001 Isobel Gamble
Illustrations © 2001 Tim Warnes
Isobel Gamble and Tim Warnes have asserted their rights
to be identified as the author and illustrator of this work
under the Copyright, Designs and Patents Act, 1988.
Printed in Singapore
All rights reserved • ISBN 1 85430 707 X
10 9 8 7 6 5 4 3

Isobel Gamble and Tim Warnes

Who's That?

Little Tiger Press

London

Daisy Dog was tired.
She made her way to
her cosy kennel for
an afternoon snooze.
But . . .

"Who's that sleeping
in my kennel?" she
yawned.

"It's Snorter Pig!
This is *my* kennel, Snorter.
It's time for you to trot off
home now."

Snorter trotted and snorted all the way home, only to discover that someone had got there before him.

"Who's that dozing in my sty?" he oinked.

Feeling very tired, Dabble swam across the pond to her nest. But two long fluffy brown ears were poking up from behind the rushes.

"Who's that snoozing in my nest?" quacked Dabble.

Racer skipped and hopped across the meadow, but he spotted a bushy tail sticking out of his cosy burrow. *Someone* was there already.

"Who's that snoring in my burrow?" he twitched.

Sandy scrambled off up a tree, looking forward to a long deep sleep. She noticed two tiny pink ears popping up between the leaves.

"Who's that snoozing in my drey?" she sniffed.

Merry scuttled back to her own little mousehole, only to discover someone *very* big and *very* furry lying right across it.

"I know who th-that is," she squeaked.

It was Merry's lucky day. Caspar was far too tired to catch mice. He slowly got up and made his way to his very own bed. But someone cute and cuddly was already sleeping there.

"Who's that sleeping beneath my favourite blanket?" he miaowed.

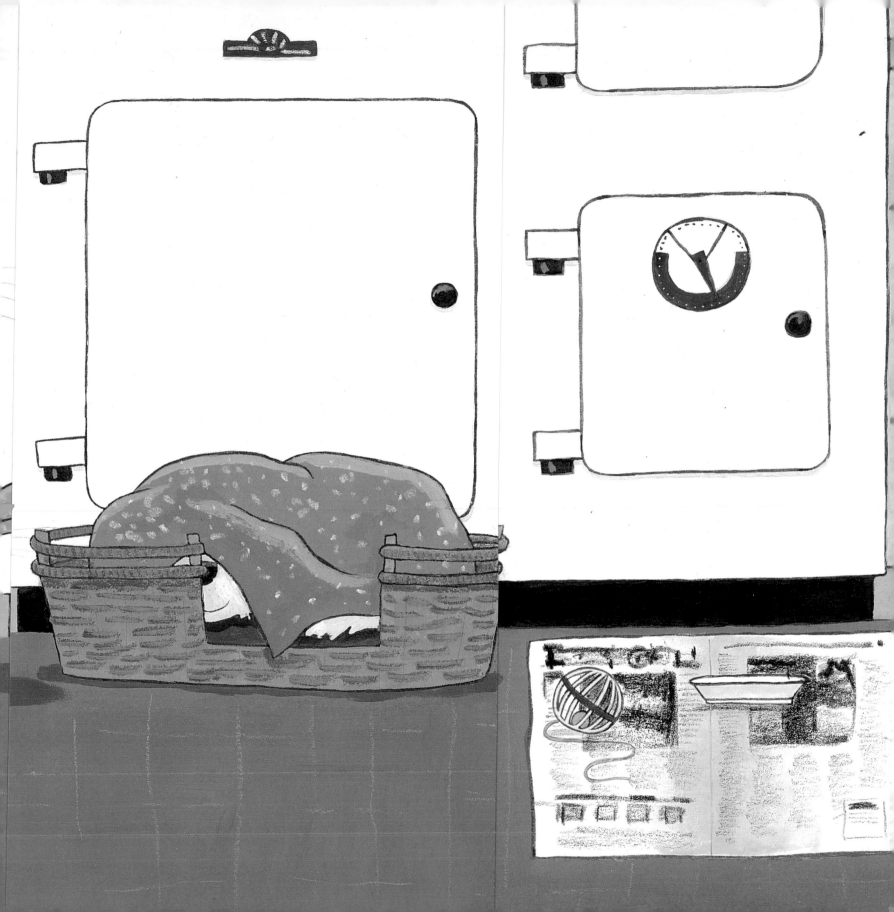

Poppy padded wearily
home. It was getting late
and she was very tired.
But . . .

"Who's that cuddled
up in my kennel?" she
yelped.

"So *there*
said Daisy
"It's long
Now off y

Alfie and Betty Bug

Amanda Leslie

Fidgety Fish

Big Bear
Little Bear

DAVID BEDFORD
JANE CHAPMAN

Read a book at bedtime

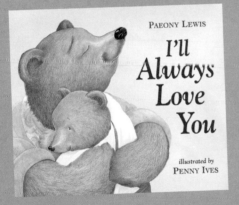

PAEONY LEWIS

I'll
Always
Love
You

illustrated by
PENNY IVES

A peekaboo riddle book

who's
that
scratching
at my
door?

Amanda Leslie

Wait for me,
Little Tiger!

Julie Sykes · Tim Warnes

For information regarding any of the above
titles or for our catalogue, please contact us:
Little Tiger Press, 1 The Coda Centre,
189 Munster Road, London SW6 6AW, UK
Telephone: 020 7385 6333 Fax: 020 7385 7333
e-mail: info@littletiger.co.uk www.littletigerpress.com